THE SUMMER

NOISY

BOOK

PICTURES BY
LEONARD
WEISGARD

STORY BY
**MARGARET
WISE
BROWN**

THE SUMMER NOISY BOOK

HarperCollins *Publishers*

Little Muffin was sleepy.
So he fell asleep in the
back of the car. And
while he was asleep his
eyes were closed. But
he heard the car go out
of the city and into the
country.

Wheeeeeeee
Past police whistles
Rurrrrrrrr
Through tunnels.
And Chug, chug, chug,
Past trains
Zip

Over bridges
And Brrrrrrrr
Down the long road to the country,
Brrrrrrrr
Up hills and down hills
Away down the long wide road.
Into the wild green country.

Muffin
could
hear the birds.
How was that?
Then suddenly
Muffin heard
Clippety Clop
Clippety Clop
Clippety Clop
Clippety
Whoa!
What was that?
Muffin stood on his
hind legs to see!
He saw it.
Whoa!
What
was
it?

A HORSE

Then all about him Muffin heard

ding   dong

ding   dong   dingle

dingle   dingle

What was that?

He leaned way
out to listen.
Cowbells on
cows at a cow
crossing.
The ringing of
cowbells.
He smelled
cows.
And then he
saw them.
All over the
grassy
meadows
Cowbells

And then
it was night.

Deep in the country as the moon shone down and the stars pricked the dark night sky, among the dry sounds of summer and the rattle of bugs, Muffin heard
peep peep
Jug a rum
Jug a rum
Jug a rum
What was that?

Peepers and frogs
in the dark cool ponds
deep in the country.

He went to sleep
that night on a farm.

And in the morning before
Muffin opened his eyes he
heard Cockadoodle Doo
It was still dark but Muffin
knew what it was—

A ROOSTER

And then way off in the barn he heard

Meowwwww
Squeak
Squeak
Squeak
Meowwwww
Squeak
Squeak
Squeak

What was
that so early
in the morning?

Muffin didn't
know. So he
got up and
went out to
the barn to see
what it was.

It was a cat

and seven little kittens.

And he heard
    Clank, Clank, Clank
Down in the warm dark
barn someone rattled
the milk pails. And he
heard the cows chewing
their cuds down in the
warm dark barn.
    How was that?
And he heard mice
scampering in the hay.
    How was that?
Then way off in the
fields he heard
    Baaaaaaaa
        BAAAAAAAA
    Baaaaaaaa
        BAAAAAAAA
        What was that?

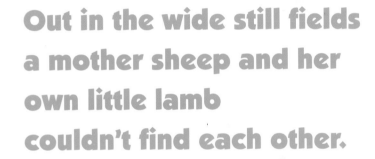

Out in the wide still fields
a mother sheep and her
own little lamb
couldn't find each other.

And then they did
Baaaaaaaa BAAAAAAAA
They found each other
and then
Wheeeeeeeeh Honk, Honk, Honk
What on earth was that?
A mother donkey he-hawed
high on a hill
as she nuzzled her baby donkey
But the little donkey was too little
to make much noise

He just kicked his little feet.
He was too little to he-haw.
He had just been born.
The calves were still asleep.
And then as the sun rose
higher in the sky
there was a little noise way up
in a tree
peck peck peck
crack crack crack
What could it be?

Three little robins popped
out of their eggs,
and then
Peep, cheee, cheeee, cheeee,

**They opened their little mouths
for their dinner.
And what did they eat?**

And then all the wild flowers bloomed
The May flowers bloomed
The dandelions bloomed
The violets bloomed
And the wild geraniums

But could Muffin hear that?

Then Muffin
heard a noise
way up in the sky
like chairs being thrown
all around the room
like mountains falling down
like a giant's stomach
rumbling.
What
could
it
be?

Was it
a
big
brass
band
crashing
their
instruments
up
on
a
cloud?

NO!

Was it—

A train roaring across the darkening sky?

Or
a fire engine
squirting
hoses
at
the
sun?

NO!

It was

A THUNDERSTORM
with thunder
and lightning—
summer lightning.

And the rain came down
on the wild flowers
and the ducks.

And there was Muffin
all safe and warm
with the other animals
in the big warm barn.